Hat Trick

by Matt Christopher

Illustrated by Daniel Vasconcellos

Little, Brown and Company

Boston   New York   London

To my great-grandson and namesake,
Matthew Christopher Howell

First Edition

Library of Congress Cataloging-in-Publication Data

Christopher, Matt.
    Hat trick / by Matt Christopher ; illustrated by Daniel Vasconcellos. — 1st ed.
        p.   cm. — (Soccer Cats ; #4)
    Summary: When his older brother gets his picture in the paper for scoring three goals in a soccer game, Stookie tries to emulate his feat.
    ISBN 0-316-10669-0
    [1. Soccer — Fiction.   2. Brothers — Fiction.   3. Teamwork (Sports) — Fiction.]   I. Vasconcellos, Daniel, ill.   II. Title.
III. Series: Christopher, Matt. Soccer Cats ; #4.
PZ7.C458Hat   2000
[Fic] — dc21   99-36649

10   9   8   7   6   5   4   3   2   1

WOR

Printed in the United States of America

Soccer 'Cats Team Roster

Lou Barnes	*Striker*
Jerry Dinh	*Striker*
Stookie Norris	*Striker*
Dewey London	*Halfback*
Bundy Neel	*Halfback*
Amanda Caler	*Halfback*
Brant Davis	*Fullback*
Lisa Gaddy	*Fullback*
Ted Gaddy	*Fullback*
Alan Minter	*Fullback*
Bucky Pinter	*Goalie*

Subs:

Jason Shearer

Dale Tuget

Roy Boswick

Edith "Eddie" Sweeny

Chapter 1

Stookie Norris sat across the dinner table from his older brother, Greg. Greg had pushed his plate aside and was reading the sports column of the local newspaper.

"A color photo, not just black and white!" Greg gloated. "Here's what the caption says: 'Greg Norris, striker for the Blue Waves soccer team, scored the league's first and only hat trick this season on Tuesday.'" He put the paper down so Stookie could see the photo, too. It showed a sweaty-faced Greg beaming for the camera.

"The guy who wrote the article says my playing was the best he's ever seen for a twelve-year-old. That my fancy footwork and speed left the other team in the dust." Greg leaned back in his chair and locked his hands behind his head. "What do you think of that, little bro?"

Stookie looked at the photo, then at his brother, and shook his head admiringly. "Wow. I wish I'd been there to see it." He handed the paper back to Greg. "But, um, what's a hat trick, anyway?"

Greg snorted. "You don't know what a hat trick is? Some soccer player you are! It's only what every striker should try to do, in every game. I can't believe your coach hasn't told you that."

Stookie reddened. His mother came to his rescue.

"Well, I don't know what a hat trick is, either. Perhaps you won't mind telling me — before you tip over in your chair?"

Greg rocked his chair forward with a thump. "A hat trick is when one player scores three goals in one game," he explained impatiently. "It's very hard to do."

"But your coach told you that's what strikers should try for, every time?" Mrs. Norris asked with surprise.

Greg groaned. "Well, he didn't come right out and *say* that. But you should have seen how pumped he was when I scored that third goal! It's pretty clear to me that that's what he wants me to do."

Mr. Norris added, "It was pretty exciting. I almost busted with pride right there in the stands." He chucked Greg playfully under the chin. "Keep up the good work."

Stookie looked at the newspaper article with envy. At that moment, he decided that he, too, would do what all strikers were supposed to do. He would do all he could to make a hat trick at the next Soccer 'Cats game.

Chapter 2

Hey, did you guys see the sports column in the paper yesterday?"

That was the first thing Stookie asked his Soccer 'Cats teammates the next day at practice. The team was gathered in the stands, waiting for the coach to arrive.

"Yeah, pretty cool picture of your brother," said Amanda Caler, one of the team's halfbacks.

"Did you read the article?" Stookie continued. "My brother is a star! He knows everything there is to know about soccer. His coach thinks he's the best. You should have heard what he said when Greg made that hat trick!" He looked from one player to another. "You *do* know what a hat trick is, don't you?"

Jason Shearer popped his gum. "Yeah, isn't that when a guy with a black cape makes a rabbit appear or turns a broken egg into a dove?" The other kids snickered.

"Ha, ha, very funny," Stookie grumbled. "Well, we'll see who's laughing when *I* get *my* name in the paper for scoring three goals next game. 'Cuz that's just what I'm going to do!"

Lou Barnes arrived in time to hear what Stookie was saying. "You're going to score three goals next game?" he echoed. "Guess I might as well hand in my soccer shoes then, because you won't need me in the front line with you."

Stookie threw a mock punch at the big striker's arm. "Well, someone has to assist me out there," he joked. "If you're lucky, I might just mention your name when the newspaper interviews me. Of course, that's supposing I don't bring the ball in all by myself each time." He locked his hands together behind his head and leaned back against the stands.

"Oh, brother," he heard someone say. But before he could identify who had said it, the coach showed up and started practice.

"Hi, team," Coach Bradley greeted them. "Let's get going. Lou, Jerry, Stookie, and Roy, we're going to practice shooting on goal today. Bucky, you and Jason are our goalies." Jason started to groan, but at a look from the coach he turned it into a cough. "The rest of you will be doing tackling and dribbling drills."

Stookie's heart soared when he heard the coach's plan. It was as if the coach had decided to help Stookie reach his goal of making a hat trick.

I bet he saw the paper, too, Stookie thought. *Greg must be right; coaches must want their*

strikers to make hat tricks. Well, I won't let Coach
Bradley down!

For that part of practice, Stookie worked harder than he ever had. Each time he faced Bucky or Jason, he sized them up carefully. Then he kicked the ball with all his might to a spot he hoped the goalie wouldn't reach in time. He faked Jason out more times than not, but Bucky was much quicker. He only made half his kicks good against the 'Cats regular goalie.

Still, when it was time to switch to another drill, Stookie was sure he'd improved. Of course, kicking a goal during a practice wasn't quite the same as during a game, but Stookie wasn't worried. Somehow, he'd make his three goals the next game. He was sure of it.

Chapter 3

The game against the Black Hawks started right on schedule the next day. Stookie Norris took his position at center field. Jerry Dinh lined up on his right. Lou Barnes was on his left.

The Soccer 'Cats hadn't played the Black Hawks before, but Stookie wasn't nervous. He had his game plan in mind and was sure he could make it work.

The 'Cats had won the toss. At the referee's whistle, Stookie gave the ball a gentle kick to Jerry. Jerry prodded it forward with his foot, picking up speed as he dribbled downfield. Stookie and Lou kept pace with him, ready to help out if Jerry got in trouble.

Sure enough, a tackler charged Jerry. Jerry saw him coming and booted the ball cleanly toward Stookie.

Now's my chance! thought Stookie. He raced forward, dribbling as fast as he could. A halfback came forward to meet him.

"No, you don't!" Stookie muttered. He sidestepped the Black Hawk, taking the ball with him. The halfback put on the brakes, but he was too late. Stookie was already five feet farther downfield and moving fast.

Now two fullbacks double-teamed him. Out of the corner of his eye, Stookie saw Lou wave for a pass. Stookie hesitated.

If I can just get past the double-team, the goal will be right in front of me, he thought. *Then it will be me against the goalie. I'm sure I can beat him!*

He decided to go for it. It took some fancy

footwork — and one little shove the ref didn't see — but he made it around the two fullbacks. Suddenly it was Stookie against the goalie, just like in practice the day before. With a mighty kick, Stookie walloped the ball to the high right corner.

Swish! Goal! Stookie jumped in the air, fist pumping. "One down, two to go!" he cheered. He looked around for his teammates, expecting them to congratulate him. But most of them just yelled hooray and started back to their positions. They didn't want to be called for delaying the game.

Only Lou had waited, and he wasn't cheering. In fact, he looked puzzled.

"Stookie, didn't you see me waving?" Lou called as they trotted back toward midfield. "I had a clean shot at the goal. You didn't."

Stookie shrugged. He didn't know why Lou was concerned. He should have remembered that Stookie was going to try for a hat trick this game. And that meant taking as

many shots on goal as he could. If Lou didn't remember, well, Stookie wasn't about to remind him. To do that would risk tipping off the defense. Lou would just have to figure it out for himself.

Meanwhile, Stookie wasn't just going to stand around waiting for plays to happen. He knew that if he was going to make a hat trick, he had to get his foot on the ball no matter what. He charged downfield to join his teammates in the fight against the Black Hawks.

Dewey London and Bundy Neel were working hard to get the ball back into Black Hawks territory. Finally Dewey stole it and sent it flying toward the sideline. Stookie took off after it like a shot.

So did Lou. The right striker reached the ball first. But instead of backing off and letting Lou handle it, Stookie stuck his foot in and tried to snake the ball away.

"What are you *doing?*" growled Lou. "Get back in your position, you numbskull!"

Numbskull, am I? Stookie thought angrily. *Who's the one who forgot today's game plan? Sheesh!*

Chapter 4

For the rest of the first half of the game, Stookie was a whirlwind on the field. He did everything he could to get and keep control of the ball. In fact, he shadowed the ball everywhere, straying out of his position time and again—and getting in the way of his fellow 'Cats. More than once, he found himself battling his own teammate for the ball. A few times, someone else had to rush to his spot to cover his position for him.

Then, just before the halftime buzzer sounded, he finally made another goal. The

Black Hawk goalie stumbled over the ball. All Stookie had to do was nudge it with his foot to send it over the line and into the net.

Stookie barely had enough energy to leap in the air. All that ball-chasing had pooped him out. Still, he hustled to the sideline at halftime. He was sure the coach was going to praise him for his efforts.

Just the opposite happened.

"I didn't think I needed to remind everyone of the importance of staying within your positions," Coach Bradley said. His eye fell on Stookie for a long moment, then moved on. "But maybe I was wrong. So let me say it again: Stay in your own lanes. Help out when needed, but trust your teammates to know what they're doing out there. They're trusting you, after all."

Stookie caught Lou frowning at him. He shrugged and looked away. His gaze fell on the stands. There, to his surprise, sat his brother!

Greg was busy talking with his best friend, Roger Charlton. As Stookie watched, Greg took a tattered newspaper from his back pocket and showed it to Roger. Roger rolled his eyes and said something to Greg. Greg made a face and shoved the paper back in his pocket.

Stookie's heart pounded. His brother had never come to one of his games before. When Greg saw Stookie looking at him, he gave him the thumbs-up sign. Then he nodded, as if to say, "I like what I see out there, little bro."

Stookie felt a warm glow pass through him. But moments later, that warmth turned stone cold.

"Stookie, you look like you need a rest," Coach Bradley said. "Roy, take Stookie's place when the second half starts."

"But Coach—" Stookie started to protest. A withering look from the coach silenced him. So when the second half started a moment later, Stookie sat on the bench. He had to watch as Roy Boswick took position at center midfield. A substitute striker!

When the action started, Stookie sneaked a peek up at the stands. He hoped his brother was watching the game and not looking at him. He needn't have worried.

Roger was still in the bleachers, but Greg was nowhere in sight.

Chapter 5

The Soccer 'Cats wound up winning the game against the Black Hawks, 3–0. Roy had scored the third goal on an assist from Lou.

"That goal should have been mine," Stookie grumbled to Lou after the game. "Can you believe the coach took me out?"

Lou was taking off his soccer shoes and putting on his regular sneakers. He shot Stookie a look of disbelief.

"What?" said Stookie.

Lou just shook his head, gathered up his

soccer shoes, and walked away. Stookie walked home by himself.

At dinner that night, Stookie waited for Greg to say something about the game. But Greg was silent except to ask if Stookie had ever made it back into action. Stookie mumbled a no, and Greg shook his head sadly. Stookie could guess what his brother was thinking: *That's no way to get a hat trick, now, is it?* The thought made him turn beet-red. So he tried not to think about it.

The next day, the sun shone bright and there was a cool breeze. It was perfect soccer weather. After breakfast, Stookie called Lou.

"Hey, buddy, want to kick the ball around for a while?" he asked cheerfully.

There was silence on the other end. Then Lou said, "Uh, I can't today. My mom, um, needs me to stick around the house this morning."

"All morning?" Stookie asked. "Well, what about later?"

Lou mumbled something about yard work and said he had to go. Stookie hung up the phone, puzzled.

Oh, well, he thought, walking from the kitchen to the garage. *Guess I'll go for a bike ride instead. Maybe I'll run into someone who can play.* He wheeled his bike outside, slung a leg over, and took off. He headed for the nearby bike path.

For half an hour he rode the bike path. He passed some older folks out walking and some kids he recognized from school, but no one from the Soccer 'Cats team. Finally, he turned back.

On his way home he decided to ride past the soccer field. Maybe one of his teammates was there and would want to kick the ball around.

As he pedaled up to the field, he could see that there *were* kids there—a lot of them. In fact, it looked as if there was a game of three-on-three going on. He picked out Dale Tuget, Alan Minter, the Gaddy twins, Jerry Dinh — and Lou.

Stookie stared with disbelief. *Guess his mom didn't need him all morning after all,* he thought.

He refused to consider the other explanation: that Lou had lied to him because he didn't want to play soccer with him. Quickly, before any of the 'Cats could see him, Stookie jumped back on his bike and rode away.

Chapter 6

Stookie coasted into his driveway. He wheeled his bike back into the garage and hung his safety helmet over the handlebars. The day was still bright and sunny, but Stookie's good mood was gone. He felt as dark and gloomy as the inside of the garage.

He was surprised to see his brother on the phone in the kitchen. Usually, this time of day, Greg was showering up after soccer practice. He was even more surprised to hear his brother shouting angrily.

"So I missed one lousy practice. I think I

earned a day off after my performance last game, don't you?" There was a long pause. "Oh, yeah? Well, if getting a hat trick isn't such a big deal, then how come no one else has done it this season? Like you, for instance?"

Greg looked around and saw Stookie staring at him; his face reddened and he shouted into the phone again. "Anyway, I don't hear Coach Williams bawling me out for not being there today. So why don't you just stuff a sock in it, Roger?" He hung up the phone with a bang, then faced Stookie again.

"Well, what do *you* want?" he demanded.

"Uh, nothing," Stookie stuttered. He couldn't believe that Greg had just hung up on his best friend. That would be like Stookie hanging up on . . . Lou.

Or Lou lying to me. The thought pierced his brain like an arrow.

Greg stalked to the refrigerator and yanked open the door. After a few moments, he pulled out the milk and poured himself a glassful. He drank it down without stopping, wiped his mouth, and *thunk*ed the glass on the countertop.

"Guess you're wondering what *that* was all about," Greg said, jerking a thumb toward the phone.

Stookie gave a half shrug.

Greg laughed harshly. "Turns out Roger is jealous of me because of that newspaper article. He said he was glad I hadn't shown up at practice today, so he didn't have to watch me hot-dog all over the field. Said that I was more concerned with personal glory than helping the team to win. Can you believe that?" Greg shook his head. "After I single-handedly led the team to victory, last game. Sheesh. How sore can a guy get? Oh, well. Who needs him?"

Greg walked into the living room, turned on the TV, and surfed through the channels. After five minutes, he clicked the TV off again.

He climbed halfway up the stairs toward his bedroom, then stopped and came back down. He paused uncertainly and finally came back into the kitchen.

"What are *you* staring at?" he muttered. "Shouldn't you be out playing with your little friends?" He stormed past Stookie to the garage. Moments later, Stookie heard him pedal away on his bike.

I should *be out playing with my friends,* Stookie realized. *But for some reason, my friends don't want to play with me. At least, one of them doesn't.*

Chapter 7

Stookie tossed and turned that night. The next day at practice, he was cranky from lack of sleep. Seeing Lou made him even crankier. Usually, he and Lou joked around before practice began. Today, the two boys stood as far apart as they could.

Coach Bradley clapped his hands to gather the team together. "I've got a new offensive play to teach you today." He asked Roy and Jerry—a substitute and a regular striker—to help demonstrate. "It's a pretty simple move, really—as long as the two players involved are in good communication. It's called a fake crossover. We'll use it when we have a direct free kick near the opponent's goal."

He placed a soccer ball on the ground. "Both players line up as though they're going to take the kick. One stands here," — he pulled Jerry five feet to one side of the ball — "the other over here."

He walked Roy farther away from the ball, on the opposite side from Jerry. The boys and the ball now formed a lopsided triangle, with the ball as the point nearest the goal.

"Now here's the tricky part," the coach said. "Jerry and Roy both start toward the ball." He set both boys in slow motion. "Jerry pulls his foot back as if he's going to take the kick — but instead of connecting with the ball, *he steps over it.*" Jerry stepped over the ball.

"A split second later, Roy takes the kick." Roy nudged the ball with his foot.

"If all goes well," the coach said, "the defense has been so busy watching Jerry that

they've ignored Roy. So Roy's kick takes them completely by surprise. Lots of times, the ball winds up in the goal. But just in case it doesn't," —he put his hand on Jerry's head—"Jerry is in prime position to follow the kick and gain control if necessary. And Roy shadows him." The two boys walked a few steps. "Okay, any questions?"

Bundy Neel raised his hand. "How do the two players know which one is actually going to take the kick? Won't they collide if they don't know?"

"Yeah," Jason Shearer added. "Some of our players can't afford any more knocks on the head!"

The coach raised an eyebrow at Jason. "Talking about yourself, Jason?" The other players laughed. "Let's come up with a signal. The person who will take the kick will raise his or her arm in the air. Okay?"

Everyone nodded.

"Let's pair off and give it a try, then. To

start, let's have strikers pair up with strikers, and then halfbacks with halfbacks. Then we'll mix it up. Rest of team, just watch for now, then we'll have you get in position."

Jerry and Roy, already paired up, stayed together. That left Lou and Stookie staring at each other.

"Well, let's get on with it," Lou finally growled. "I suppose you'll want to take the kick. After all, making a goal is what you Norrises live for, right?" He kicked the ball to Stookie, then turned away.

Chapter 8

Stookie and Lou had never played together so poorly. They kicked each other's shins, tumbled over each other's feet, and even collided so hard they fell flat on their backs. When the coach finally signaled for them to switch partners, Stookie was bruised and angry. His play improved with his halfback partner, Dewey, but his mood did not. He couldn't wait for practice to end.

But when it did, Coach Bradley asked Stookie and Lou to stay for a moment.

"Okay," he said, hands on his hips. "What's going on between you two?"

Stookie looked sullenly at Lou, who stared at the ground. Since Lou didn't answer, Stookie did.

"Lou's jealous of me."

Lou's head shot up. There was fire in his eyes. "*Jealous* of you?" he cried. "What for?"

"Because I've come closer to scoring a hat trick than you have!" Stookie retorted. "And everyone knows that's what every striker should do!"

"Who told you that? Your big brother?" Lou rolled his eyes. "Just because he got his name and picture in the paper doesn't make him an expert on soccer. Oh, he's a good player and all, but I heard he's been kind of a jerk since that hat trick. In fact, I heard he might get kicked off the team for missing practices. And even his best friend can't stand to be around him anymore, because all he

talks about is his hat trick, hat trick, hat trick." Lou shook his head. "And you want to be just like him? Unbelievable."

Stookie was stunned. He turned to the coach.

"But, getting three goals in one game means . . . means . . ."

"Means you could be hogging the ball and not letting anyone else take shots on the goal," the coach quietly finished for him. "Which is just what you did in the game against the Black Hawks—and why you spent the second half on the bench instead of on the field."

He sighed. "Stookie, if there's one thing I want all my players to learn, it's teamwork. There's no room for superstars on the Soccer 'Cats. That's why none of my plays focuses on one particular player. Instead, each play gives more than one 'Cat a chance of helping the team to win. Take the fake crossover, for instance."

Stookie hung his head. The coach hadn't yelled at him, but he might as well have. Stookie felt awful.

"Lou," he said. "I'm sorry for the way I've been acting. I didn't realize I was being such an idiot. What can I do to make it up to you?"

Lou chuckled. "Don't sweat it." Then he looked thoughtful. "Well . . . maybe there is something you can do."

"What? What?" Stookie asked eagerly.

"Stick around and work on the fake crossover with me some more. We really stank at it today!"

Chapter 9

Stookie and Lou walked home together forty-five minutes later. Stookie was sweaty and tired, but happier than he'd been all week.

In fact, he was feeling so good, he decided to try to talk some sense into Greg. He'd hate to see his brother lose his best friend the way he'd almost lost Lou.

He needn't have worried. When he walked into the house, he found Greg and Roger sitting together at the kitchen table.

"Okay," Greg was saying, the grin on his face a mile wide. "I'll admit I've been a jerk for the past few days, if you'll admit that my scoring a hat trick was the best soccer playing you've ever seen in your life."

Roger threw up his hands in defeat. "Fine, fine. I bow down before your greatness." He flopped his arms down onto the table. "Now get dressed for practice, you big jerk. You're lucky you're still on the team, you know."

Greg turned serious. "I know. If I hadn't called the coach to apologize as you suggested, I bet I'd have been kicked off for sure. Thanks for talking sense into me, buddy."

Just like Lou did for me, Stookie thought. He headed upstairs, thinking about how lucky he and his brother were to have such good friends.

Stookie bounded out of bed the next day, eagerly looking forward to the game against the Tadpoles. He hoped he and Lou would have a chance to run the fake crossover play.

The game started promptly at ten o'clock.

Stookie took his position at center field. When the ref's whistle blew, he kicked the ball to Lou. Lou tore up the grass, dribbling with all his might toward the Tadpoles' goal. Stookie and Jerry kept pace with him.

Lou came face to face with a tackler and shunted the ball back to Stookie. Stookie started down the field but met a Tadpole half-back. A quick glance to the right told him Jerry was open. He aimed a pass in that direction. But before he could get the kick off, a second Tadpole defender stole the ball from him.

Rats! Stookie thought, spinning around to give chase. *Where did that guy come from?*

Fortunately, the Tadpole was better at steal-ing than he was at dribbling. Bundy Neel got the ball away from him easily. With an expert pass, he sent it back to Stookie. Stookie con-trolled it, then took off like a shot.

He crossed over into Tadpole territory, dodging a halfback, then a fullback. All of a sudden, the goal was right in front of him. Heart pounding, he drew his foot back to take a shot on goal.

Wham!

The same Tadpole who had stolen the ball hit him from behind. Stookie landed hard.

Tweet!

The ref called for a direct kick. Stookie stood up and shook himself off. As the Tadpole defense lined up in a solid wall before the goal, Stookie caught Lou's eye. Now was their chance to try the fake crossover!

But which player would take the kick, Stookie or Lou?

Chapter 10

After a moment's hesitation, Lou raised his hand, signaling that he'd take the kick. The ref placed the ball on the ground where the foul had taken place. Stookie took position a few feet to one side of it. Lou moved into his place.

Stookie charged forward. Lou did the same. Thanks to the extra practice they'd put in the day before, they moved like a well-oiled machine. Stookie stepped over the ball. He shielded Lou for just a split second. But that was all Lou needed to trick the defense.

Whap! Lou's foot connected solidly with the ball and sent it soaring past the wall of full-backs. The goalie made a frantic dive, but he was too late. Goal!

Lou and Stookie leapt into the air, whooping and slapping palms. Not five minutes into the game and already they were on the score-board!

"Great shot, Lou!" Stookie yelled.

"It's your turn next, buddy," Lou responded.

But the score stayed at 1–0 for a while. Then, ten minutes before the end of the first half, the Tadpoles scored on a corner kick.

"The game's not over yet!" 'Cats captain Bundy Neel cried, as they took their positions.

"You've got that right!" Stookie agreed loudly. At the ref's whistle, he set the ball in motion. Passes flew across the field from Lou to Stookie to Jerry and back again. Slowly but steadily, the front line powered their way past the halfbacks into Tadpole territory.

But the Tadpoles weren't about to let them

go unchallenged. When Stookie received the ball from Jerry, two fullbacks double-teamed him. The other fullback and a halfback were covering Jerry and Lou. Stookie didn't have anyone to pass to!

He heard Dewey London call to him from behind. With a desperate stab of his foot, he pulled the ball away from the Tadpoles. There wasn't time or room to turn around to pass to Dewey. So instead, Stookie kicked with the heel of his foot and sent the ball rocketing blindly backward!

The fullbacks were caught completely by surprise—and out of position. Dewey didn't even have to move. He just kicked the ball into the goal!

"Yes!" Dewey screamed. "I made a goal! I made a goal!" The usually quiet halfback was jumping for joy.

The half ended with the score 2–1. The team crowded around the coach, sucking orange slices and downing cups of water.

"I like what I see out there," Coach Bradley praised. "Good teamwork and good thinking on your feet. Fancy footwork out there, mister," he added, grinning at Stookie. "That move will give you a check mark in the assist column."

Stookie grinned back, then pretended to turn thoughtful. "Hmm. Assists are almost as good as goals, aren't they?" He tapped a finger against his chin. "Let's see, if I set a team record for assists *and* score a hat trick, why, that should be enough to earn me a full color picture on the front page!"

"You even think about it," Lou growled menacingly, "and the next time we try a fake crossover you'll find yourself flat on your back."

Stookie laughed and threw an arm around Lou. "There are worse things in life than having a friend who keeps a person in line."

Lou gave Stookie a shove and the two boys fell over in a heap, laughing.

SOCCER 'CATS

#1   The Captain Contest

#2   Operation Baby-Sitter

#3   Secret Weapon

#4   Hat Trick

Join the Matt Christopher Fan Club!

To become an official member of the Matt Christopher
Fan Club, send a business-size (9½" x 4") self-addressed,
stamped envelope and $1.00 (in cash or a check
payable to Little, Brown and Company) to:

Matt Christopher Fan Club
c/o Little, Brown and Company
3 Center Plaza
Boston, MA 02108